TWIST AND SNOUT

TWIST AND SNOUT

a guide to pigging out on life

**Art Opportunities, Inc.,
and
Patrick Regan**

Andrews McMeel
Publishing

Kansas City

Twist and Snout: A Guide to Pigging Out on Life copyright © 2003 by Art Opportunities, Inc. All rights reserved. Printed in China. No part of this book may be used or reproduced in any manner whatsoever without written permission except in the case of reprints in the context of reviews. For information, write Andrews McMeel Publishing, an Andrews McMeel Universal company, 4520 Main Street,
Kansas City, Missouri 64111.

ISBN: 0-7407-2681-1

Library of Congress Control Number: 2002111553

03 04 05 06 07 WKT 10 9 8 7 6 5 4 3 2 1

ATTENTION: SCHOOLS AND BUSINESSES

Andrews McMeel books are available at quantity discounts with bulk purchase for educational, business, or sales promotional use. For information, please write to: Special Sales Department, Andrews McMeel Publishing, 4520 Main Street, Kansas City, Missouri 64111.

INTRODUCTION

In the summer of 2000, the city of Cincinnati went hog-wild for pigs. The Big Pig Gig was a community-wide public art event celebrating Cincinnati's heritage as the one-time center of the nation's pork-packing industry. But while the event had ties to the city's history, the real purpose of the pig party was pure fun. Local artists dressed, painted, decorated, and creatively transformed more than four hundred fiberglass pigs that took up temporary residence in public places all around downtown Cincinnati and across the border in northern Kentucky. By all accounts, the Big Pig Gig was a squealing success. In the spirit of that irresistible barnyard hero, this little book offers a snootful of wise and witty advice on how to pig out on life.

TWIST AND SNOUT

It's so easy to get caught up in the mundane details of life. We're only human, after all. Maybe that's the problem. Maybe, we should be more like . . . pigs!

TWIST AND SNOUT

Pigs remind us NOT to take ourselves too seriously,

TWIST AND SNOUT

TO RELAX
and
stay cool,

TWIST AND SNOUT

to keep life simple,

TWIST AND SNOUT

and to regain the sense of *adventure* we had as kids.

TWIST AND SNOUT

As we grow older, we're told that we must be **DIGNIFIED** at all times.

TWIST AND SNOUT

Hogwash!

TWIST AND SNOUT

The truth is that it's fun to ham it up now and then.

TWIST AND SNOUT

After all, who says you can't live

HIGH

on the hog

TWIST AND SNOUT

and still bring home the bacon?!

TWIST AND SNOUT

So what if we get a little *risqué* now and then?

TWIST AND SNOUT

(It's hard to be a *divine swine* all the time.)

TWIST AND SNOUT

The **important thing** is not to try to be something **you're not**.

TWIST AND SNOUT

Yes, sometimes life gets a little prickly.

TWIST AND SNOUT

And occasionally we all feel like we're **stretched** a little thin.

TWIST AND SNOUT

But don't wallow in despair

TWIST AND SNOUT

or insulate yourself from the world.

TWIST AND SNOUT

Make a **STATEMENT** AND **STAND UP** for yourself!

TWIST AND SNOUT

And remember, sometimes when you're feeling down, a little retail therapy does just the trick.

TWIST AND SNOUT

Keep dreaming big!

TWIST AND SNOUT

And keep believing in the power of your bright ideas.

TWIST AND SNOUT

**Love
your
country,**

TWIST AND SNOUT

but explore new lands, too.

TWIST AND SNOUT

Embrace
the future,

TWIST AND SNOUT

and never
 underestimate
the power
 of a big,
friendly smile.

TWIST AND SNOUT

Adopting the *way of the pig* can help us all enjoy life more,

TWIST AND SNOUT

whether you're the type

who likes to blend in

TWIST AND SNOUT

or who likes

to be a

little more

BOLD.

TWIST AND SNOUT

Whether you like to get dressed to the swines

TWIST AND SNOUT

or prefer to keep it casual,

TWIST AND SNOUT

these are

the days of

swine and roses,

my friend.

TWIST AND SNOUT

So think like a pig, and remember:

TWIST AND SNOUT

LIFE IS A *banquet,*

TWIST AND SNOUT

a celebration,

TWIST AND SNOUT

a grand performance.

TWIST AND SNOUT

Don't forget
to dance.

Artist Credits

p. i: "Country Ham Pig," Lynn Rose
p. ii: "Pigliacci," Christine M. Bieri
p. 3: "Pig Pals," Sarah Lahti
p. 5: "Hamlite," Margaret Wenstrup
p. 7: "Porky Play'a," Students of Bill Thomas, Woodward High School
p. 9: "Un Cochon Dans Le Jardin," Paula Ott, Denise Strasser, Sally McLane, and Susan Koenig
p. 11: "I Squeal, You Squeal, We All Squeal for Ice Cream," Ms. Heather K. Bollen and Indian Hill Middle School Art Students
p. 13: "Reginald, Dressed to the Swines," Michael Chaney
p. 15: "Hog Wash," Jill Dehner
p. 17: "Porker's Wild," the U.S. Playing Card Company Art Department
p. 19: "Hog Wild," Cindy Hackney
p. 21: "Bringin' Home the Bacon," Bradford McDougall
p. 23: "Sexy Sow," Heather Chitwood

TWIST AND SNOUT

p. 25: "Divine Swine," Fabricia Duell
p. 27: "Porkemon," Wayne Clark
p. 29: "Porkupine," Zoe Hutton and Catherine Duffy
p. 31: "Pulled Pork," Richard Groot and the Deskey Staff
p. 33: "Pig-Tac-Toe," Jonathan Hand
p. 35: "Stainless Squeal," Jonathan Hand
p. 37: "Go Veg Piggy," Betsy Reeves
p. 39: "Saksy Babe," Mark Adams and Bruce Raitch
p. 41: "The Messenger," Sam Hollingsworth
p. 43: "Idea Hog," Frederic Ellenberger
p. 45: "Uncle Ham," Heather Chitwood
p. 47: "O Sowlo Meeeeeo," Stephen Geddes
p. 49: "2 Sowsend," Joshua Thomas
p. 51: "Cheshire Pig," Steve and Rokeya Brauch
p. 53: "Jiggin' Piggy," Cindy Matyi
p. 55: "Dandelion Swine," Amanda Hogan
p. 57: "Foodie Tootie in the Land of a Sowsand Foods," Mary Ann Lederer

TWIST AND SNOUT

p. 59: "Juicy Lucy in the Sky with Diamonds," Dodie Loewe
p. 61: "The Three Little Pigs: House of Sticks," Jan Marx Knoop
p. 63: "Days of Swine and Roses," Linda Kreidler
p. 65: "Albert Swinestein," Barbara Fabing
p. 67: "Maisownette," Lynne, Scott, and Steve Hamons
p. 69: "The Silky Sow with Ham Bag," Floral Designers of the Silky Way
p. 71: "Swine Lake (Hoofanova)," T. A. Boyle
p. 73: "Swine Lake (Odile)," T. A. Boyle

Photographer Credits

Principal photographer: Javier E. Jarrin
Additional photographers: Tony Arrasmith, Robert A. Flischel, Thomas W. Guenther, Joe Harrison, Connie Liebel, Peggy McHale, Kelly Barnhorst-Schelle, and Chris Cone